Published 1984 by
The Hamlyn Publishing Group Limited
London · New York · Sydney · Toronto
Astronaut House, Feltham, Middlesex, England
© Mansell Print Limited 1984

ISBN 0 600 38946 4

Printed in Italy

Frosty Frolics

By Simon Joyner

Hamlyn

London · New York · Sydney · Toronto

Winter had arrived early in Misty Wood. Thick swirling mists hid the trees and large snowflakes fell from the sky and covered the ground in a blanket of white.

Gilbert Mouse had been caught in the storm as he was hurrying home. Luckily, Oswald Owl had spotted him and carried him high up into the shelter of an old pine tree.

Not far away in Chestnut Hollow, Minnie
Shrew sat snugly in her warm cottage. She was
busy knitting a jumper for Henry Hedgehog.

'Where is Henry?' asked Gordon Grub.

'He's out catching the lights,' Minnie said
mysteriously.

Gordon was just wondering what that could
mean when . . .

The door blew open and in staggered
Henry, looking very wet and cold.
   'Dear me,' he said, his teeth chattering.
'It's certainly not the night for hedgehogs to
be out of doors.'

'Did you catch the lights, Henry?' Minnie asked, giving him a quick brush down.

'In the end,' Henry said, enjoying the chance of a free scratch. 'It's always the way. As soon as the dark winter nights come they all hide from me, naughty things, and it takes hours to find them again.'

He walked to the door and shouted:

'RIGHT, YOU LOT, IN YOU COME. QUICK MARCH, LEFT, RIGHT, LEFT, RIGHT!'

'You're worse than a sergeant major, Henry,' grumbled the glow-worms. They didn't enjoy being caught and used as lamps – but at least they only had to do it in Winter.

They cheered up a little when Henry tried on his jumper. In fact they all laughed rudely.

'Oh, you do look handsome in that, Henry,' said Minnie, ignoring the glow-worms.

The jumper was a little on the large side, but Henry didn't like to complain.

Minnie was so pleased with the jumper she rushed over and gave Henry a great big hug.

'I say!' said Henry, turning pink with embarrassment.

The next day, the storm had cleared.
Winter sunlight sparkled on the crisp white
snow. The animals decided to spend the day
playing outside. Minnie brought along a big
box full of sweet chestnuts to roast.

The snow had brought down lots of branches and the grubs collected some twigs and lit a fire so they could roast the chestnuts.

But, just when there was a nice blaze going, a gust of freezing cold mist came along and put it out.

'Henry, how do we start it again?' asked the grubs.

'Don't you know anything?' Henry said crossly. 'What you have to do is blow on it.'

So all the grubs took a deep breath and blew as hard as they could.

'Thanks very much!' spluttered Henry,
covered in soot.

After Henry had brushed all the soot off his new jumper, he went to see what Minnie and the other grubs were doing. 'Whoever is that creature playing with Minnie?' he wondered as he hurried towards them.

When Henry got close he realised that the mysterious stranger, who stood grinning at him, was made of snow!

'Do you know who he is?' asked the grubs, trying not to laugh. 'It's you – it's a snowhog!'

'Humph!' snorted Henry. 'That ugly thing looks nothing like me.'

Then the strangest thing happened. The snowhog began to move. Was it alive after all?

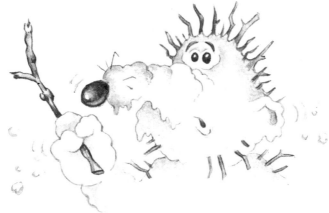

Bonk! It hit Henry on top of his head!

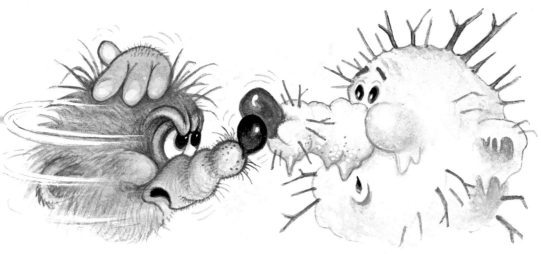

'Who did that?' cried Henry, spinning round angrily. Then, *thud!* It happened again.

'It *is* alive!' shouted one of the grubs. 'Our snowhog has come to life!'

Just as everyone was about to turn and run . . .

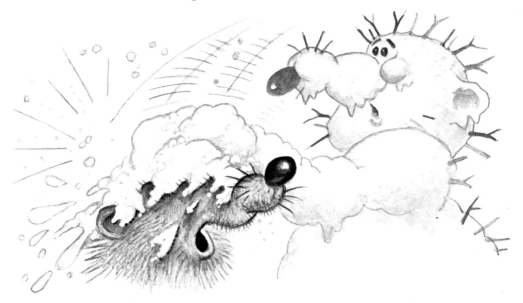

The snowhog shook and trembled and who should pop up through his neck but Mole!

'What are you all staring at?' he asked. 'Anyone would think you were looking at a ghost.'

When everyone had got over the shock, they all laughed. Trust Mole to pop up right in the middle of their snowhog!

Suddenly Minnie said, 'Oh, I almost forgot. It's time for Gilbert's surprise. Come on, everyone.'

So they all went to the frozen pond in the middle of the wood. When they arrived, however, Gilbert Mouse was nowhere to be seen.

'Oh dear!' whispered Minnie, getting a bit worried. She knew that a frozen pond in the middle of winter was no place for a little mouse to be alone.

Then, just as everyone began to get really worried, they heard a voice shout: 'Hurrah! The show begins.' And, from behind a clump of frozen bulrushes, out leapt Gilbert on skates.

He landed gracefully on the frozen pond and put on a wonderful ice-skating show, complete with twirls, spins and twists. How his audience clapped and cheered.

Gilbert whizzed about on the pond, first on one leg and then on the other.

'And now for my grand finale,' he announced, going into a dizzy-making spin.

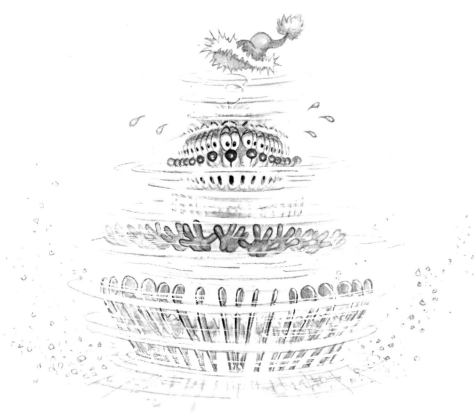

Gilbert spun round and round, going faster and faster until his nose and ears were just a blur. All at once, with a loud splash, Gilbert completely disappeared!

Gilbert's audience weren't quite sure what to do. Was this part of the show, or was Gilbert in trouble?

They waited . . . and waited . . . for him to appear, but no Gilbert. At last they walked carefully over to the neat little hole that Gilbert had left in the ice and peered in.

'I think he sharpened his skates too much,' said Henry. 'We must rescue him quickly.'

Eventually, they managed to pull Gilbert
out. He felt as cold as – ice!

Back at Minnie's warm cottage, Gilbert sat
in front of her roaring fire to defrost.

That evening everyone sat round the
fireplace chuckling about the day's events.
As the logs crackled in the hearth,
snowflakes began to tap on the windowpane.
How lovely it was to be sitting indoors in
Minnie's snug cottage.